LAKE CLASSICS

*Great American
Short Stories III*

❧❧❧❧

Wilbur Daniel
STEELE

Stories retold by Prescott Hill
Illustrated by James Balkovek

LAKE EDUCATION
Belmont, California

LAKE CLASSICS

Great American Short Stories I

Washington Irving, Nathaniel Hawthorne, Mark Twain, Bret Harte, Edgar Allan Poe, Kate Chopin, Willa Cather, Sarah Orne Jewett, Sherwood Anderson, Charles W. Chesnutt

Great American Short Stories II

Herman Melville, Stephen Crane, Ambrose Bierce, Jack London, Edith Wharton, Charlotte Perkins Gilman, Frank R. Stockton, Hamlin Garland, O. Henry, Richard Harding Davis

Great American Short Stories III

Thomas Bailey Aldrich, Irvin S. Cobb, Rebecca Harding Davis, Theodore Dreiser, Alice Dunbar-Nelson, Edna Ferber, Mary Wilkins Freeman, Henry James, Ring Lardner, Wilbur Daniel Steele

Great British and Irish Short Stories

Arthur Conan Doyle, Saki (H. H. Munro), Rudyard Kipling, Katherine Mansfield, Thomas Hardy, E. M. Forster, Robert Louis Stevenson, H. G. Wells, John Galsworthy, James Joyce

Great Short Stories from Around the World

Guy de Maupassant, Anton Chekhov, Leo Tolstoy, Selma Lagerlöf, Alphonse Daudet, Mori Ogwai, Leopoldo Alas, Rabindranath Tagore, Fyodor Dostoevsky, Honoré de Balzac

Cover and Text Designer: Diann Abbott

Library of Congress Catalog Number: 95-76754
ISBN 1-56103-072-4
Printed in the United States of America
1 9 8 7 6 5 4 3 2 1

CONTENTS

❦ Lake Classic Short Stories ❦

"The universe is made of stories, not atoms."
　　　　　—Muriel Rukeyser

"The story's about you."
　　　　　　—Horace

Everyone loves a good story. It is hard to think of a friendlier introduction to classic literature. For one thing, short stories are *short*—quick to get into and easy to finish. Of all the literary forms, the short story is the least intimidating and the most approachable.

Great literature is an important part of our human heritage. In the belief that this heritage belongs to everyone, *Lake Classic Short Stories* are adapted for today's readers. Lengthy sentences and paragraphs are shortened. Archaic words are replaced. Modern punctuation and spellings are used. Many of the longer stories are abridged. In all the stories, painstaking care has been taken to preserve the author's unique voice.

Lake Classic Short Stories have something for everyone. The hundreds of stories in the collection cover a broad terrain of themes, story types, and styles. Literary merit was a deciding factor in story selection. But no story was included unless it was as enjoyable as it was instructive. And special priority was given to stories that shine light on the human condition.

Each book in the *Lake Classic Short Stories* is devoted to the work of a single author. Little-known stories of merit are included with famous old favorites. Taken as a whole, the collected authors and stories make up a rich and diverse sampler of the story-teller's art.

Lake Classic Short Stories guarantee a great reading experience. Readers who look for common interests, concerns, and experiences are sure to find them. Readers who bring their own gifts of perception and appreciation to the stories will be doubly rewarded.

❦ Wilbur Daniel Steele ❦
(1886–1970)

About the Author

Wilbur Daniel Steele was born in North Carolina. He was raised in Denver, Colorado, where his father was a college professor. Many of the men in the Steele family were clergymen, but Wilbur Daniel wanted to be an artist. As a young man, he went east to study painting in Boston. Later he attended art schools in Paris and in Italy.

In Europe, Steele began writing short stories. He had so much success that he decided to make a career of writing rather than painting.

Steele saw much of the world. He visited the West Indies in 1916–1917. In 1918, during World War I, he served as a naval correspondent stationed off the coasts of Ireland, England, and France.

From 1919 to 1920 he lived in Bermuda. Then he traveled to North Africa and to France and England again.

In 1919, Steele was presented with the O. Henry Memorial Award for his story "For They Know Not What They Do." In the course of his career, he won this award for three other stories as well. He also wrote several one-act plays. With his second wife, Norma Mitchell, he wrote a full-length drama.

For many years Steele lived in the old Massachusetts towns of Provincetown and Nantucket and in Charleston, South Carolina. His later years were spent in Connecticut. Usually he wrote four or five hours a day, turning out stories that the *New York Times* described as "deftly mingling beauty and cruelty."

Steele described himself as "pretty much the common or garden variety of person." But one critic called him "the master of a complicated bag of tricks."

Read on to sample a few of the tales from Wilbur Daniel Steele's bag.

For They
Know Not
What They Do

What's the Kain family's
terrible secret? In this
haunting tale a young man
learns the shocking truth
about his father's dark past.
Is it too late for his mother
to save him?

CHRISTOPHER COULD NO LONGER HEAR MADNESS IN THE
CELLO'S LOW TONES.

For They Know Not What They Do

Christopher Kain told me his story late one night. We were sitting in his dressing room at the concert hall. He sat there staring into the light. His dark hair framed his pale face. His shoulders hung forward. His long, lean fingers held the neck of "Ugo"—his cello.

Christopher never knew his father. His mother, Agnes Kain, was a lady. She was quiet, sweet, and kind—a gentlewoman. As he grew up she often told him about his father, Daniel Kain. The tale grew as the boy grew. She told Christopher about Daniel, his father, and Maynard,

11

his father—and of another Maynard before him. Christopher knew he would have to be a man among men to measure up to that family. He must grow up to be strong, serious, and thoughtful. He must be kind. He must be brave. He must live up to the high standard of the Kain men.

All through his boyhood he lived with that family legend in mind. And he also lived in the matter-of-fact world of Concord Street. The two did not match.

Christopher was not strong or brave. He often saw things in the dark that frightened him. His thin shoulders tended to droop. The hours of practice on his violin left him pale.

And he wasn't always so serious, thoughtful, and kind. There were times when he lost his temper. And times when brief attacks of anger came over him that left him sobbing, sick, and weak. His mother would not look much like a gentlewoman then. Instead, she'd look like a prisoner sentenced to die.

One time he saw her like that when he had *not* been angry. That day, he had come into the house unexpectedly. A stranger was just leaving. The man was dressed all in brown. In one hand he held a brown hat. In the other he held a cane. He had a long face and sad gray eyes.

Nothing about the man stood out. But it was not the stranger that troubled Christopher. It was the look on his mother's face. That, and the nervous way she acted. After the man was gone she spoke to Christopher in a hurry. "He came about some papers, you know."

"You mean our daily newspaper?" Christopher asked her.

"Yes," she told him. "Yes, yes."

Neither of them said anything more. That evening, Christopher broke one of his long silences. He brought up a subject that was always near to both of them.

"Mother, you've never told me *where* it is. I mean where it is on the map."

She was reading a book. She did not look up.

"I—Chris—I—I haven't a map in the house," she said quickly.

He didn't press the matter. Instead he

went out into the backyard and sat under an oak tree. After a while he forgot about the stranger's visit.

He was growing up.

Not long after that he went away to boarding school. With him he took a picture of his adored mother. He also took the memory of his dark, strong family. His attacks of anger went along with him too. And, of course, he brought his violin. At school they thought he was strange.

One fall term, five children at school got sick. The people who ran the school were afraid that others might catch the sickness. They closed the school for a week. So Christopher started home for an unexpected holiday.

On his way home he stopped at the junction to change trains. There he saw his mother! She was seated in the downtown train that was stopped there. He quickly boarded it.

She did not see him until he came walking down the aisle of her coach. He smiled at the chance to surprise her.

"Why, Mother, where are you going?"

he asked. "I'm about to have a week off—
and you're going away?" His voice trailed
off when he saw her look of horror. The
color drained out of his face and he drew
back from her. "What is it, Mother?
Mother!"

Agnes Kain opened her pale lips. "Get
off before it's too late, Christopher. I
haven't time to explain. Go home. The
maid will take care of you. I'll be back in
a day or so. Kiss me now, and *quickly!*"

He did not kiss her. He was too
shocked, too hurt. Without a word he ran
out to the platform. He watched her train
start to move and then he jumped back
aboard on the last car. After a two-hour
ride, she got off. Taking care not to be
seen, he got off, too.

An old man was waiting for her in a
carriage. Christopher kept out of sight
in the roadside trees as he followed the
carriage. He stayed far back, keeping
track of the dust it made.

He walked for miles. As he came to the
top of a hill, a view of the sea took him
by surprise. He was expecting more

farmland. For an instant he was confused. A strange sickness seemed to come over him. He had to rest a moment by the side of the road.

As he sat there, tears began to roll down his cheeks. He didn't know why. He got up. For the first time he noticed that there were gravestones all about him in the grass! The one nearest him had words carved on it. He read it aloud:

MAYNARD KAIN, ESQUIRE
1809—1839
This monument erected in his memory
by his sorrowing widow
Harriet Burnam Kain

It was his family's graveyard! He looked at another of those worn stones:

Here Lie the Earthly Remains of
MAYNARD KAIN, JR.
Born 1835—Died 1863
For the Preservation of the Union

One after another, the old white stones stood up like the bones of the dead. The only sound Christopher could hear was the rustle of the grass.

In the faded light the excited boy looked about quickly. At last he found what he was looking for.

DANIEL KAIN
Beloved husband of
Willoughby Kain
Born 1860—Died 1886
Forgive them
for they know not what they do

At that point in his story, Christopher sighed deeply. Then he told me that he left the graveyard repeating those words to himself: "Forgive them for they know not what they do." What strange words! What could they possibly mean?

* * *

Darkness now blanketed the hill. Agnes Kain stood in the open doorway of the house below. She heard something.

"Oh, Mother! Mother!" a voice cried. The boy was coming through the gate in the hedge. "Mother! It's Chris! Aren't you surprised?"

She had no answer.

"Mother! Look! I'm here!"

"Yes," she breathed. "I see."

Then he threw his arms around her. He felt her shaking from head to foot. But he didn't notice that she was trying to hide her terror. She turned to the old man beside her. "Christopher, this is your father's servant, Nelson."

Then she led the boy through the house of his family. He might have been a stranger, someone with a guidebook in his hand. He stood in the big main room, staring up at paintings. They were the men his mother had told him about.

At last he stood before the portrait of Daniel Kain—his father. The face in the picture was dark and thin. Like all the other Kains, his father's eyes seemed to shine with an inner fire.

Then Christopher came to a door. He threw it open with the happy laugh of a discoverer. But before his mother could say anything, his laughter died.

A sick man lay on a bed in the room. His face was colorless and still. His eyes were open, but they did not move.

"Oh, I'm so sorry. I didn't know!" Christopher whispered, ashamed that he had barged in.

Closing the door quietly, his mother explained. The man was the caretaker, Sanderson. He was dying. That was why she had come here—to see about some papers. "Some papers," she repeated. Christopher had to understand. . . .

Christopher *did* understand, but he was bothered by it. In this newly discovered world, he wanted to forget the matter-of-fact world of Concord Street. But the sick man reminded him of it. For it was the same man he had seen in the doorway months ago. He was the man dressed in brown, with the hat and cane.

By bedtime, though, he wasn't thinking much about the sick man. His mind was filled with thoughts of the Kains. For the first time, he felt like a part of the legend. He explored his room before he fell asleep. He touched old books and vases and pictures with care. Then he came upon a leather case in a corner. A cello was in it. The boy had seen cellos before—they looked something like smaller bass violins. But he had never touched one. When he lifted it from the case, he felt a tingle in the pit of his stomach. He touched the C-string and the tingle grew stronger.

I, myself, have heard "Ugo" sing. I know what Christopher meant when he said that the sound did not come *out* of the instrument, but rather *into* it. That night it seemed to come from all the walls and corners of the chamber. The tone was slow and rich—like the surf, heard on a far-off coast. Another touch of the strings and it sounded like drums, still farther off, or the feet of marching men. In his imagination, Chris could see their dark, shining eyes. They were the Kain men.

Christopher didn't hear his mother's footsteps in the hall. But suddenly she was standing in the open doorway. For a moment they stared at each other. Again she had that awful look on her face. Little by little the boy's cheeks grew as white as hers.

"What is it, Mother?"

"Oh, Christopher, Christopher . . . Go to bed, dear."

He didn't know why, but suddenly he felt ashamed and a little frightened. He blew out the candle and went to bed.

* * *

The next afternoon was sunny and the world was quiet. Christopher lay on the grass. He listened to the "clip-clip" of Nelson's shears as he trimmed the hedge.

"Was my father strong?" he asked.

"No, not very," Nelson said. "But when he was *that* way, five strong men couldn't hold him. I'll say that. No, if they had to go after him with a shotgun that day, it was nobody's fault. Guy Bullard saw Daniel there on the sand. He had an ax in his hand and there was foam on his lips. The children were cornered between the cliff and the water. Guy's own baby was one of them. He knew the sickness of the Kains—everybody did. It was his duty to pull the trigger on Daniel."

Nelson was much older than he looked. His mind had grown tired. Sometimes he forgot where he was, and to whom he was speaking.

"No, I can't blame Guy Bullard," the old man continued. "Nor can I blame the men who killed Maynard, Junior, the night after Gettysburg.

"It was a mercy to the both of them—father and son. And Old Maynard, Senior, too. He went easier. He got it into his head that he could walk on water. He drowned, of course.

"The only man I blame is Bickers. He was the one who told Daniel about the family problem. From that day, you see, Daniel began to take it on.

"I saw it myself. There was young Daniel, bright as you please. He didn't know there was anything wrong with the blood of the Kains. Not until Bickers told him. Then Daniel changed. It was like he'd been sentenced by a judge. He was never the same again."

The old man suddenly looked at the

shears in his hand. He had forgotten what he was doing. "Dear me," he said to himself. "One thought at a time is enough!" He fell to work again.

The steady "clip-clip-clip" moved slowly along the hedge. Not once had the old man realized that he'd been talking to young Christopher Kain.

* · * · *

Later in the day, the boy brought the bow across the cello strings. It sounded like thin laughter. He laughed, too, but not happily. His mother had told him a lot about the Kains. But she had never mentioned one thing—the madness in the blood. He smiled without joy. A wave of anger came over him as he heard his mother's footsteps in the hall.

How he hated her! It was not his father he hated, but her. She had lied to him. And he hated the man who was dying in the room below. Who was that man? Why had he come to Concord Street that day? It was another of his mother's secrets.

Christopher thought of finding and

attacking the man. The very idea made him sick. The next thing he knew he was on the floor, weak and crying. He crawled back to his bed.

Later his mother came in. "Oh, Chris! You're sick!"

"Yes," he said. "Yes! Yes!" Then he shouted, *"Go away!"*

"No, no," his mother said. "You're making yourself sick, Christopher—all over nothing. If only I could tell you—"

"Tell me what?" He began to scream. *"Go away! Go away!"*

This time she obeyed. She didn't care, he thought bitterly. She was sneaking off downstairs—oh, yes, he knew where.

If only he had a weapon—an ax! He would show them! Suddenly he felt strong, incredibly strong! Five strong men could not hold him.

Then he laughed. Oh, yes, he could stop her from going down there. If he wanted to, he could bring her back, begging.

"Tell me what?" he said to himself, laughing madly. *"What?"* And then he dropped into a deep sleep.

The next night he found himself outdoors, seated on his father's gravestone. He knew then what Daniel Kain had felt—and Maynard Kain before him. It must have been a hatred for all the dull people in the world. Those who never knew the passion of madness. Christopher hated those people. They would never know how *different* he was. He wanted to get back at them all.

Later, Christopher went into the main room with all the paintings in it. There, lying on his back, was the sick man. Only now he was dead.

And there was his mother, kneeling beside the casket. Beside her was "Ugo," the cello. Christopher felt that his mother had forgotten him. He looked up. The painting of Daniel Kain was turned to the wall!

For a moment, his mother didn't seem to know he was there. Then she turned to him. "I'm sorry, Christopher. I never meant for you to know!"

He stared hard at the face in the

casket. It was long, dark, and thin like his own. Then he turned to his mother. "Who *is* this man?" he demanded.

"Don't look at me so!" his mother said. "*Don't*, Chris!"

"Who is this man?" he repeated.

"He grew up with me," she said. "We were meant for each other, Chris. We were always meant to marry—always, Chris. But he went away, and I married your—I married Daniel Kain. Then this man hunted and searched until he found me here.

"He stood by me through that awful year," she went on. "We were meant for each other, John Sanderson and I. He loved me more than poor Daniel ever did or could.

"He loved me enough to throw away his life. Long after everyone else was gone, he stayed here. He stayed here alone with his cello and his one little memory of happiness.

"And I loved him enough to—to—Christopher, don't look at me so!"

His eyes were filled with anger. "So

this was my father," he said. "And yet you would have kept on lying to me! If I hadn't found you here now, you would have gone on lying. You would have stood by and watched me—well—go crazy. Yes, go crazy, thinking I was—well, thinking I was *meant* for it! And all to save your precious—"

Now she was crying again. "But you don't know what it means to a woman, Chris! I gave you a father with a sound mind. Can't you understand?"

He shook himself. "No," he said. Then his eyes turned to the wall beyond and the faces there. They were the Kain men. He would not lose them. He refused to be robbed of what was his right by birth—even the madness.

He reached for the cello. "It's not his!" he cried. "It's mine! It's—it's—*ours!*"

Then he turned and ran upstairs, carrying the cello with him.

Now he struck on the full strings. And he listened—breathless. But no longer did he hear madness in its tone. Something was broken, something was lost. The mad Kains had cast him out. He was no blood of theirs.

He sat on the edge of the bed and wept. Outside he could hear gentle rain falling on the roof overhead. It made a long, low melody as it fell softly on the trees. Then he realized that the melody was coming from "Ugo," the cello—and *he* was playing it.

Christopher and his mother left the house the next day. She went home. He went back to school. For part of the way, they rode together. They didn't speak much. The boy needed time. His mother had meant everything to him. Now it was hard for him to even look at her.

As for Agnes Kain, she did not look at Christopher, either. During the whole train ride, she stared at her hands in her lap. She seemed very tired. At the last minute, she spoke to him before he got off to change trains.

"Christopher," she said. "Try not to think ill of me. When you're older, perhaps you'll understand what I did."

That was the last time he ever heard

her speak. He saw her just once again—
two days later. But the telegram was
delayed and his train was late. When he
finally stood beside her bed, she said
nothing. She looked into his eyes for a
long while—and died.

* * *

After he finished telling me his story,
Christopher Kain sat motionless, his
shoulders fallen forward. His long
fingers were wrapped around the neck
of the cello. I thought he had quite
finished. But then he went on.

"And so she got me through those
years," he said. "Those nip-and-tuck
years that followed. She got me through
by her lie." I wondered what he meant,
but I said nothing.

"Insanity is a queer thing," he said.
"There's more of it about than we ever
dream. It is hidden in so many things—
in hobbies, arts, philosophy. Music can
be a kind of insanity, I know. I control
mine through my music."

"*Yours?*" I said.

"Yes, mine. I know the truth now—now that it's safe for me to know. I was down at that village again a year or so ago. I really *am* a Kain, of course—one of the crazy Kains. John Sanderson was born in the village. He lived there until his death. But my mother hardly knew him. People said he had been away from there only once in his life. That was when he took some papers to the city for my mother to sign.

"He was a caretaker at the Kain house for the last ten years of his life. And the people in the village told me something else, too. They said that before she married my father, my mother had been an actress. An actress!

"Someone had heard she was a *great* actress. Dear God, if they could only know *how* great! When I think of the scene she played out that night! It *killed* her—but it got me over the wall—"

❧

Out of Exile

Two brothers are bitter rivals for the love of the same young woman. Which one will she choose? Or will they *both* end up losing her?

MARY FINALLY CAME UP WITH A PLAN FOR CHOOSING
BETWEEN THE BROTHERS.

Out of Exile

Of course I have many memories of my boyhood on Urkey Island. But the story that stands out is the one about Mary Matheson and the Blake boys.

I still remember Mary as I saw her that night. She was standing in the sand dunes above the wreck of the "India ship." Rolldown Nickerson was there, too. The old beachcomber was carrying a strange piece of polished wood.

Mary's bridegroom was waiting in a church back in Urkey Village.

The whole thing had begun years before. It started when I was too young to understand much of it. But even at the age of six, I had heard that Mary Matheson was a fool. Everyone in Urkey Village talked about her.

Both of the Blake brothers had been courting her, you see.

I was coming home from school just at dusk. I had almost reached the corner at Drugstore Lane when I heard a voice. It was the voice of my cousin Duncan. He was the only father I ever knew. He was also the constable of Urkey Village, the one person in charge of the law.

"Drop it, Joshua! Drop it now, or by heavens—" I heard Duncan saying.

I could see only Duncan's back. But I could plainly see the faces of the others. Even though the blue shadow of the hill was falling across the village, the sky was still bright. To this day, I never see that light without feeling a shiver. For that was the first time I ever saw the deadly anger of grown men.

My cousin was speaking to Joshua Blake. Joshua held a pistol in his hand. It was an old, single-ball dueling pistol.

It had belonged to his father. His face was white with anger. The sharp Blake features seemed to stand out stronger than ever.

Andrew, his brother, stood facing him three or four paces away. He was the younger of the two, the less favored, the more sensitive.

Andrew had a few freckles sprinkled across his high, flat cheeks. And he had what no one else in Urkey had then— two gold teeth. He'd lost his real teeth in a boating accident. His gold teeth were showing now as his lip curled back. Like his brother's, his face was white with anger. Andrew's hands were empty. But he did not look defenseless.

Behind the two men was Mary Matheson. She stood in her doorway. Her hands were clutched at her throat. Her eyes were wide with fear.

The three of them seemed to be frozen in place.

"Drop it, Joshua!" Duncan's voice rang out loud and clear.

Joshua's eyes went down to the gun in

his hand. He shook his head slightly, like a sleeper waking up. At Duncan's command, he stuck the gun in his pocket.

Then I saw Duncan looking at me. Not wanting any trouble, I ran home as fast as I could.

There was serious talk in town that night. Some people said the argument between the brothers was all Mary's fault. She should have picked one of them long ago and "sent the other one packing."

That's what Miah White said, sitting in our kitchen that night. And that's what Duncan said as he paced back and forth, shaking his head. That's what almost everybody in town was saying or thinking.

The next day Mary came up with a plan for choosing between the brothers. It was a foolish young girl's plan. She told everyone about it at Alma Beedie's birthday party.

She said she'd marry the Blake boy who first brought her a gold ring. That made everyone laugh. The nearest jeweler was in Gillyport. To get a ring, the boys would have to sail across the sound and back.

Some of the young people who were there remembered later that Joshua laughed along with the others. But his brother Andrew left the house, turning at the door to look at Mary before he went out into the night. Afterward people said his face was sickly white.

Everyone thought he had gone out for just a moment. But Andrew Blake never returned to that party. The first hint of what was up came from Rolldown Nickerson, the beachcomber. A while after Andrew left, Rolldown came running in, dripping wet from the storm. He had come to tell Joshua to look out for his brother. Not knowing about Mary's plan, he thought Andrew had gone out of his head.

"Here I come onto him down by the water," Rolldown said. "He was putting up the sail on his boat. 'What are you up to, Andrew?' I said. And he said with a kind of laugh, 'Oh, I'm just taking a little sail for other parts.'

"Imagine that—with this terrible storm coming on," Rolldown said.

Then a look came into Joshua's eyes. It was a look that none of them had ever seen before. He stood there for a moment, motionless and silent.

Rolldown was at him again. "You'd better stop your brother," he said.

"Oh, I'll stop him!" Joshua said. Then throwing on his coat, he went out.

The next thing you knew all the young people had trooped down Herman Street to the shore. There, under the light of the moon, they saw that Andrew's boat was gone. And all they could see of Joshua was a shadow—sailing off in *his* boat. They called out to him, but he didn't answer. Before long he was gone, lost in the black heart of the night.

Now, a boy of six gets lonesome in the dark of a stormy night. The house shakes and the wind howls. I spent from two o'clock until dawn that night under the kitchen table. Miah White and his brother Lem were in the kitchen. They'd come to talk with Duncan.

All the three of them could say was "My heavens! My heavens!"

The next day, folks were walking the beaches, looking out on the stormy sea. Others climbed the hill for a better view. But in that storm, they got none.

Mary Matheson watched from her little house. And that's where she was when Joshua Blake came back. After all that waiting and watching, no one saw him land on the beach. Mother Polly Freeman, the west-end midwife, saw him in town. At first she thought he was a ghost from the bottom of the sea. His wet clothes were stuck to his body. There was seaweed in his hair. His face looked as cold as fish flesh. When he spoke, she thought he was crazy.

"I've got it!" he cried, taking hold of her arm. Then opening a cold, wet hand, he showed her the gold ring.

"See, I've got it, Mother Polly!" he cried again. She said he looked as if he had seen the devil face to face. Then she saw him hurry off toward Mary Matheson's house. Mother Polly said she followed him there and waited outside Mary's fence. She heard him pound on Mary's door. Then she saw Mary's face in the open window.

Joshua looked up at the window. He said nothing, but he held up the ring for her to see. After a moment Mary opened her lips. "Where's Andrew?"

That made him angry. "*Here's* the ring! You see it, Mary! You gave your word and I took it. Only God knows what I've been through. Now come! Put your things on and bring your mother if you like. We're going to Minister Malden's to be married now! Do you hear me, Mary? I'll not wait a moment longer!"

"But where's *Andrew*?" she asked him again.

"Andrew? *Andrew?* Why the devil do you keep on asking for Andrew? What's Andrew to you—now?"

"Where is he?" she said.

"Mary, you're a fool if you don't know where Andrew is," Joshua said.

"He's gone," Mary said.

"Gone, yes! Why do you keep asking?" Joshua cried.

"I knew he was gone," she said. "He told Rolldown he was going to other parts. But I knew it even before that. I knew when he turned at the door and looked at me, Joshua. He might as well have said, 'If *that's* love, then I'm going off somewhere and forget it.'"

The deadness went out of her voice. "Joshua, he's got to come back! If he doesn't, I can't bear it. I gave you my word—I'll marry you. But only when Andrew comes back to stand at the wedding. He's got to—*got* to!"

Joshua stared at her, his mouth hanging open. Then he turned away without a word and walked off.

It is impossible to tell in a few words what the next ten years did to those two people. Most of the people in town blamed Mary. The gossips spoke of Joshua's hang-dog look. "And why shouldn't he look so?" they said. "A man can't stand being made a fool of. . . ."

Miah White was always talking about

the trouble that Mary had caused.

One night, he told my cousin Duncan, "Something must be done."

"About what?" Duncan said.

"About Josh and her. It ain't right. I saw him on the beach last night. He looked like a ghost. He kept saying, 'Who's to pay the bill? Who's to pay the bill?' No, sir! It ain't right!"

"But what *is* to be done?" Duncan said.

"God knows!" Miah said. "But the girl made a promise. She should keep it! That 'India ship' stuff is just a foolish game she's playing."

Duncan smiled and shook his head. There was no sense arguing with Miah once he got started.

There had been a lot of talk in town about the "India ship." The night Andrew vanished, there had been a ship off shore. It looked like an east-bound clipper. Later, Mary said that Andrew had often talked of sailing on it. Over the years she had come to believe that he had done it after all. What better way for a man to go into exile?

When the townspeople doubted it, she had an answer. Had anyone ever *seen* Andrew's boat go down? And no one had seen what happened to his body. Not with their own eyes. It was much later when his boat washed up on shore—empty. The matter seemed to rest there.

By the time I was nine or ten the whole tragic episode had gone out of my head. Sometimes I would meet Mary Matheson or Joshua Blake on the street. In a dim sort of way, I knew that the two were "engaged."

It was a few years later when I had a sudden and moving reason to remember that long-buried drama.

I had been away to Highmarket Academy for two years. Now I had come home for summer vacation. Three days later, as I strolled through the village graveyard, I saw Mary Matheson. She was a beautiful woman of 30 then. But the look on her face was angry.

In Urkey it was the custom to put up a stone for a man lost at sea. On that day Mary was standing by such a stone.

It had been put up for Andrew. It seemed clear that she had not seen it before.

At the sight of it she cried, "No, no! They're still trying to kill him—all of them are! But they won't! They *won't*!"

A moment later, I noticed Joshua walking through the graveyard. He was watching Mary from a distance. When he spoke, his voice sounded dry and cold.

"So, Mary, you're at it again?" he said.

"But they won't!" she said again. She seemed to take flame. "It's not right! They've done this just to mock me, and I know it. But I don't care. They won't say that he's dead—they won't!"

"Mary," said Joshua, all the anger of the years flooding into his voice. "Mary, I think it's time you stopped being such a fool. We've all had enough of it, Mary. Andrew is dead."

She turned on him with a swift, accusing challenge. "You say that now? You *know* that now? Perhaps you've seen his body washed up on one of the beaches—just today? Why so late, Joshua? If you knew, why couldn't you have spoken out ten years ago—or five years ago? *Why?*"

"Because—"

"Yes, because? Because?" she said. "Say it now, Joshua—that you know for sure that Andrew went down. I dare you!"

Joshua said it. "I know for sure that Andrew went down that night."

"*How* do you know?" Mary cried. "Did you see him go down? Tell me that!"

For a moment Joshua said nothing. Then he cried out, "Yes! Yes, I saw Andrew go down that night. I heard him call out in the dark. I saw his face in the water. I saw his hand reach up, up through a crashing wave. I could almost touch it—but not quite. Now here I stand and say it out loud. I couldn't reach his hand—not quite. . . . So I've told you, Mary, what I swore I'd never tell. . . . *Curse you!*" And with that, he turned and ran off toward the town.

Mary started after him. "Joshua!" she called. "Joshua, come back!" But he did not seem to hear her.

Then I hurried off myself.

Soon after, it was announced that Mary Matheson was going to marry Joshua Blake—at last. Joshua seemed like a changed man now. The old, hard mask was gone. He actually wore a smile as he walked through town.

So the wedding day came. The sky was red that morning. Folks worried that a storm was brewing. But the sea stayed calm. There was a ship on the horizon that barely seemed to move. Yet it was growing larger as it got nearer. It made some folks think of the "India ship" that Mary used to talk about.

By about five o'clock, the ship had sailed around to the western side of the island. That seemed strange. With a storm coming on, that was the worst place to be. And the storm did come. It hit just before the wedding was to start.

What a disaster! The street lamps were pale yellow blurs. The wind howled and the rain poured down. And before long there was worse news than just the bad weather. The ship we had seen that day had run aground. Now it was breaking up on the other side of the island.

Outside the drugstore, I heard the news in the voices of men I couldn't see.

"*Aground?* Where?"

"On the outer bar—at the south end of the outer bar, they tell me."

The voices came and went, whipped by the wind.

"What boat was it? One from the village?"

"No—that ship."

"Not that—that—*India ship?*"

"Yep—that India ship."

I hurried across the island through the terrible wind and rain. At last I ended up on the western beach. But I didn't know exactly where. I only knew it was a frightening place to be alone. A big wave running up the beach almost knocked me down.

It was carrying a huge timber. I wondered if it had come from the "India ship." That got me to thinking of the poor men who must be aboard her.

If the hour I spent crossing the island seemed a minute, time now seemed to move slowly. Then, as I slowly crept along, I was suddenly taken by surprise. Standing there before me was Rolldown Nickerson, the beachcomber.

He was loaded down with junk he had gathered up in the dark. He had empty bottles, wooden floats, and other such rubbish. As he walked, he'd drop one thing and pick up another.

I decided to follow him. From time to time I tripped on the things he threw down. For some reason I bent down to pick up something he dropped. I could feel in the dark that it was made of polished wood. There was some kind of carving on it, too. The thing seemed empty, until I shook it. Then I could hear a kind of rattle inside.

I caught up with Rolldown, shouting over the roll of the wind and surf, "What do you make of this, Rolldown?" I held up the wooden thing.

He took it from me, dropping half his rubbish in the act. Then he shook it. "Got something into it," he said.

"Yes, I know," I said. "Now let me have

it back, if you don't mind, Rolldown."

"Something hefty," he continued. I noticed he had dropped the rest of his load and now clung to my treasure. "It could be valuable!"

"But it's mine, I tell you!" I cried.

"No it ain't," he said.

He was walking faster to shake me off. Our shouting, angry voices rose higher in the wind.

"It's *mine!*" I yelled. "Give it to me!" And I grabbed at his arm again. He let out a squeal and shook me off. Then he ran up the face of the sand dune that overlooked the beach. I followed right after him.

At the top of the dune, both of us saw her—Mary Matheson. How she got there I don't know. But it didn't matter. There she stood, as still as a statue.

It looked as if she had been standing there for hours instead of minutes. In a way it seemed that she had been there for all those ten long years—waiting for the "India ship" to return.

Just then I heard Rolldown Nickerson

cry out. When I turned his way I saw him throw the wooden thing to the sand. Then he ran off into the darkness.

The thing landed by Mary's feet. She didn't seem to notice it.

Then I heard another cry. I ran in that direction, and saw that Rollover had bumped into Miah White. As was often the case, Miah had been drinking. I had no time to deal with him. So I turned back to find Mary, but she was gone.

For a while I wandered in the blinding rain. Finally I headed back to the village and went to the church. Rolldown was already there. He stood outside in the street. His face was pale as putty. Over and over he was asking, "You seen it? You seen what I seen?" But no one paid attention to him.

Inside the church, the women of the village had gathered. The only man there was Joshua. He stood in the farthest corner. One of the women said he'd been looking out the window for hours.

Then he suddenly turned from the window and showed us his face. Once more it was the face we had known for so many years. His look was dry and bitter again, his lips pressed thin with hate. Then he looked beyond us, over our heads, at the corner where the door was.

There, framed in the doorway, stood Mary Matheson. She didn't look at us, but only stared at Joshua. She seemed dazed, like a sleepwalker. Then we heard her speak.

"He's come!" she said in a clear, loud voice. "Andrew's come back again." Still she stared at Joshua. He did not move or say a word.

"Do you understand, Joshua?" Mary asked. "Andrew has come back for the wedding. Now I'll marry you—*if you wish*."

Joshua did not speak, nor did the anger on his face change. But now he came walking up the length of the aisle. Mary waited for him at the door. There was a strange smile on her lips.

Joshua halted before her. Folding his hands behind him, he looked her over slowly from head to foot. "You lie!" That was all that he said to her.

"Oh, no, Joshua. I'm *not* lying. Andrew has come for the wedding.'

"You lie," he repeated. "You know that you lie, Mary. You know as well as I do that Andrew is dead."

"Yes, yes—" She said, looking down at something tucked under her shawl. "But I didn't say—" Then she removed the shawl and held up the object she had been hiding. It was the thing Rolldown had thrown away. It was the thing I had picked up and been robbed of. It was the thing that had seemed, in the dark, like something made of polished wood.

Oh God, no! It was the skull of Andrew Blake! The hard bone had been polished by sand and sea. What I thought were carvings were the teeth. Now the two gold teeth shone in the candlelight of the church. After all these years, the skull had been washed ashore by the storm. And to think that I had carried it, and felt it, and not known what it was!

Now it lay in Mary's hand. It paid no attention to any of us. Its empty eyes

stared up at the ceiling. And Joshua—
the brother—made no sound. His face
had turned a curious color, like a green
thing sprouting under a stone. His knees
caved a little under his weight. As we
watched, we saw his hands moving over
his own chest. And then we heard his
voice, croaking out in a horrible whisper.
"Turn it over!"

Mary said nothing. Nor did she move
to do as he said. It was like some awful
game of cat and mouse, the way she
quietly stood and watched him.

"Mary—do as I say now—turn it over!"
Joshua said again.

But still she made no answer; nor did
she obey.

Then Joshua's voice turned harsh. He
cried out, "Give it to me! It's mine!" Then
he rushed toward her, reaching out for
the skull.

But my cousin Duncan stepped in his
way and sent him flying.

Joshua continued on, running out the
church door. All the while he was
laughing in a horrible, unearthly way. It

was such an awful sight that we all just stood there. We looked over at Mary Matheson. Her face was still set in that same strange smile. It was as if she didn't know that tears were streaming down her cheeks.

"Let him go," was all she said.

But they didn't let him go for too long a time. The crowd had already seen the stamp of death on the man's face. When they finally looked for him, they found him lying on the grass by Lem White's gate. He was stone cold dead.

I shall never forget the look of him in the lantern-light. And I'll always remember the look of them that crowded around and stared down at him. My cousin Duncan looked puzzled. Miah White looked angry. And the three black men from the wrecked ship looked confused. It had not been an India ship at all. It was a coffee carrier from Brazil.

Now I remembered the long-forgotten question that the dead man had once asked. "Who is to pay the bill? Who is to pay the bill?"

Well, both men had paid the bill for a light-hearted girl's word. But I think that Mary Matheson has paid the most. For she has had longer to pay. Still she lives alone in her little house. Of course, she is an old woman now.

But I am almost forgetting the answer to it all. I hadn't so long to wait as most folks had. When I got home to our kitchen that night, I found my cousin Duncan already there. The lamp was lit. I came in softly because of the lateness. That's how I happened to surprise him. And that's how I got to see what he had before he could hide it.

I don't know yet how he came by it. But there on the kitchen table lay the skull of Andrew Blake. When I took it in my hand and turned it over, I found out what Joshua had meant. There was a hole in it. It was clean and round.

I remembered something as I looked at that skull. I had heard a rattling when I shook it back at the beach. Now I peeped in through the round hole. There I could make out the shape of a bullet. It was nestled loosely between two points of bone behind the nose. I guessed that it was a bullet from an old, single-ball dueling pistol.

Joshua Blake had played with such a pistol many years back. No doubt he had taken it with him to Alma Beedie's birthday party. And there was no doubt at all now that he had carried it with him later that night—when he went looking for his brother Andrew.

The Yellow Cat

What *really* happened
aboard the deserted ship?
Was there foul play of some
kind? And why did the crew
leave the cat behind? Read
on to find out.

THAT EVENING I ROWED OUT TO THE *ABBIE ROSE*. I
WANTED TO SEE THE MYSTERY SHIP FOR MYSELF.

The Yellow Cat

I once had the chance to board a deserted ship. Not that she was a *dead* ship. Oh, no. She was a good ship, a sound ship, even a handsome ship. She sailed across as blue and shining a sea as I have ever known. There was no single thing you could pick out that looked wrong about her. But as soon as I saw her, I knew that no hand was on her wheel.

The name of that ship was the *Marionette*. I remember how quiet and eerie it was when we boarded her. The sun was hot that day, but the silence on her deck made me shiver with cold.

On board we found a parrot in a cage. That was the only living thing there.

There was a table set for four. Nowhere was there any sign of disorder. But to this day, no one knows what became of the captain and crew.

Sometimes years will go by without a case of this sort. And then, in a single year, several will turn up. You'll read about them in small articles tucked away in the back of the newspaper.

That is where I read about the *Abbie Rose*. The headline said: "Abandoned Ship Picked Up At Sea."

The story read as follows:

"The first hint of another mystery of the sea came in today. The schooner *Abbie Rose* arrived, manned by a crew of one. The outbound freighter *Mercury* sighted the *Abbie Rose* off Block Island on Thursday. The ship was acting in a strange manner. When the crew of the *Mercury* boarded the *Abbie Rose*, they found no one there.

"Everything was in perfect order and in good condition on the *Abbie Rose*.

Except for a yellow cat, the ship was deserted. The lifeboat was still on board.

"No signs of disorder were seen in any part of the ship. The stove in the galley was still warm to the touch. Everything was in its proper place. But the ship's log was missing.

"Captain Rohmer of the *Mercury* put two of his men aboard the *Abbie Rose*. They sailed it back to this port.

"The two men were Stewart McCord and Sven Bjornsen. McCord brought the ship in this noon, after a very rough voyage of five days. He reported that Bjornsen had been blown overboard while checking one of the topsails.

"McCord himself showed evidence of hardships of the voyage. He seemed to be a nervous wreck."

Stewart McCord!

It happened that I used to know the fellow. In fact I had been quite friendly with him in the old days. I remembered him as a solid sort of a person. He had not struck me as a fellow who would be bothered by his nerves.

And there was another strange thing about the story. I always keep track of the weather reports. I knew there had been no rough weather during the past week. So how could Bjornsen have been blown overboard?

That evening I rowed out to the *Abbie Rose*. I wanted to see it for myself. But it was hard at that time of night to see anything but a black blotch on the water.

I called out, "McCord! Oh, McCord!"

A voice came back, "Hello! Hello, there—ah—"

The man's voice sounded a bit uneasy.

"It's Ridgeway," I said.

"Ridgeway—" He repeated my name. He still sounded uneasy. Then McCord looked down at me.

"Oh," he said brightly, "it's *you*. I'm glad to see you, Ridgeway. By heavens! I'm glad to see you!"

I tied my rowboat to his ship and climbed aboard.

"Come into the cabin and have a drink," he said. Then he clapped me on the shoulder. That struck me as odd. In the old days McCord hadn't been the shoulder-clapping sort.

The ship's cabin was about nine feet square, with bunks on one side. On the other side was a door to the stateroom. Another door led into the galley.

For some strange reason, it all seemed familiar. I looked into the galley and noticed a rusty hook in the ceiling. Suddenly a memory came back to me.

I said, "Was there anything hanging from this hook? A parrot, maybe?"

"What do you mean?" McCord asked.

"Do you know anything about this schooner's history?" I asked.

"No," he said. "Why?"

"Well, I do," I said. "For one thing, she's changed her name. Fourteen years ago she was called the *Marionette*. She was deserted then, too."

McCord leaned forward. His face was almost colorless. "I am not surprised," he said. "What I've seen and heard—" He lifted his fist and brought it down with a sudden crash on the table. "Let's have a drink!" he said.

He went into the stateroom and came back with two glasses and a bottle. He filled the glasses and pushed one towards me. He swallowed the contents of the other and sat down.

"A parrot?" he said. "No, this time it was a cat. A yellow cat. She was—"

"*Was?*" I said. "Where is she?"

"Vanished. I haven't seen her since the night before last. That's when I caught her lowering the lifeboat—"

"*Stop it!*" It was I who banged the table this time. "McCord, you must be drunk," I said. "*Drunk*, I tell you. A *cat*? You're letting a *cat* throw you off your head like this! She's probably hiding somewhere below deck this minute."

"Hiding?" he said. He regarded me for a moment with a strange look. "I guess you don't know how many times I've been over this ship. I've checked every corner from top to bottom."

"Maybe she fell overboard," I said. "Like this fellow Bjornsen did. And by the way, McCord—"

"What do you know about Bjornsen?"

he demanded suspiciously.

"Well—only what I read in the paper,"
I told him.

"Hah!" He said. Then he changed the
subject. "I found the ship's log."

"You did, eh? From the newspaper I
guessed that there was no sign of it."

"I just found it last night, under the
mattress in the stateroom," he said. He
picked up a big book from the table.

"It's not so much a log, really. More like
the captain's personal record," he went
on. "He put things in it you wouldn't put
in a ship's log." McCord shook his head.
"For one thing, that man hated the
Chinese."

"The *Chinese*?" I said.

"Yes. The ship's cook was Chinese."
McCord opened the book and began to
read: "'Anything can happen to a man at
sea, even a funeral. Especially to a
Chinese, who is of no use. They are
barbarians, as I look at it.'"

McCord looked up. "That gives you an
idea of how he thinks."

He turned to another page. "Here's

more: 'I'll get that sneaky Chinese! You never can hear him coming in those slippers of his. Tonight I turned around and found him standing right behind me. He could have stuck a knife into me easy! I rapped him on the ear. That will make him walk louder next time!'"

McCord looked up again. "Do you get an idea of the fellow?"

"Oh, yes," I said. "I know the type. Even though this Chinese fellow has him beat by 30 centuries of civilization, he calls him a barbarian. But a man like the captain has got to have someone to feel superior to. . . . "

"You're right," McCord said. He lifted the book again. "And then we read about another chap going to pieces—a man named Peters. On August 3 he refused to eat his dinner. He said he'd caught the Chinese making passes over the chowder-pot with his thumb."

I shook my head.

"Well, at any rate, the disease seems to be catching," McCord said. "The next day it's Bach, the second seaman. Listen to this: 'Bach says he is being watched. He says the Chinese has got the evil eye. Says he can see you through the wall. Why don't you take care of him?' I tell Bach. Bach says nothing, but he goes over to his bunk and feels under the mattress. He comes back looking strange. 'By God!' he says. 'The devil has swiped my gun! There's going to be real trouble aboard this ship.'"

"The *evil eye*?" I said. "Sounds to me like those people feel guilty about something. That's why they blame the Chinese for spying on them."

"Maybe not," McCord said. "I can see how that Chinese might have been peeking at them. Look at it this way. He's out on the water with all these crazy people. They're hitting him on the ear. They're looking around for guns, and so on. Wouldn't you be keeping an eye on people like that?"

I nodded.

"There's one more entry after that," McCord said. "'This is the end! My gun is gone, too. We've got do something soon.

Bach says there's more ways than one to do it. And that's what I think, too!'"

McCord closed the book. "See, Ridgeway? The rest is blank paper."

"Well, that's one 'mystery of the sea' solved," I said. "The so-called 'barbarian' got *them* before they could get *him*."

"And threw the bodies over the side?" McCord said.

"Probably," I said.

McCord looked thoughtful. "You think they came back and got the barbarian? Then they threw *him* over the side, eh? There were none left, remember?"

He had me there. "I guess I don't know," I said.

"I do," he said. "The Chinese *did* put them over the side. And then, after that, he died—of wounds in his head."

"So?"

"Remember, the skipper didn't ever mention a cat in his log," McCord said.

"Why in thunder should he mention a cat?" I said.

"True, why *should* he mention a cat? But there's a reason why he should *not* mention a cat. That's because there was no cat aboard at the time."

"Oh, all right," I said impatiently. Now I was sure McCord was drunk.

He leaned toward me. "That cook would have been from the south of China, probably." McCord seemed to be talking to himself. "There's a lot of that belief down there. It's a strange business—this shifting of souls—"

I'd had enough of McCord's foolish talk. I picked up the bottle and threw it through the open doorway. I heard it splash in the water.

"Now, either you come ashore with me, or lie down and get some sleep," I said. "You're drunk, McCord. Do you hear me?"

"Ridgeway," he said, speaking very slowly. "You are a fool if you can't see better than that. I'm *not* drunk. I'm sick. I haven't slept—and now I *can't*."

He suddenly jumped up and shouted, "You don't understand what I've been through!"

He paused for a moment and then went on. "What do you think became of

Bjornsen, eh? Listen! It happened on the first night after we took over this ship. I'd been at the wheel all day. It wasn't a hard task. We had good weather, and the ship was pretty much sailing herself.

"Bjornsen took the midnight shift, and I turned in. But I didn't drop off for quite a spell. I could hear his boots overhead as he walked back and forth.

"I was just falling asleep when he came into the cabin. He said, 'The wind is dying down. I wonder if I should put a little more sail on her.'

"I was so sleepy that I didn't care, and I told him so."

"'All right,' he says. 'I'll just shake out one of them topsails.'

"Then I heard him say, 'Scat, you—! This cat is going to drive me crazy! She follows me around everywhere.'

"He gave a kick. Then I saw something yellow fly out through the cabin door into the moonlight.

"I slept for about four hours. When I woke up, I went up on deck to see how Bjornsen was doing.

"He wasn't at the wheel. I called out for him, but got no answer. Then I took a lantern and looked all over the ship. I couldn't find a sign of him. Then I saw the cat. She sat by the wheel, washing her face. I noticed a scar on her head. It looked new, only about three or four days old. The sight of that cat was creepy in the moonlight. I ran over and grabbed her. I meant to throw her overboard. You have to understand how upset I was.

"Now you know how a cat will act when you grab it like that. But this one didn't. She just began to purr. I dropped her on the deck and backed off. You remember Bjornsen had kicked her—and I didn't want anything like that to happen to—"

McCord turned on me with a sudden anger. "You don't believe me! You're so *sure* of everything. But I'd just like to have seen you out there! All alone, and a shipmate—" He stopped talking then and stared into space.

"Go on," I told him.

He looked at me again. "The next day, I felt better. I even fed the cat. There was no breeze all day, so I wasn't busy. I slept a while on the deck—a little nap.

"That night a steady breeze came up. I set the sails and tried to get a little rest without falling asleep. I was thinking something might come up—a storm or the like. But I think I must dropped off. I remember hearing sounds from the galley, and I hollered, 'Scat!'

"A little later I looked up and saw something really strange," McCord said. "It was the shadow of a tail on the deck. Then I saw the solid part of the animal— its shadow, I mean. It was round, and it looked like it was hanging from the top of the doorway. But that didn't make sense. How could she hang there—done up in a ball like that?

"I got out my gun. Just then that shadowy thing twisted itself around. In a flash, right on the floor before me, was the shadow of a man's head—upside down. A man's head with a Chinaman's pigtail hanging down!"

McCord went over to the door and pointed. "I fired, and here's where my bullet hit. I ran up on deck and there I saw it. It was right next to the main mast, crouched down. It started sneaking off very slowly. I started firing again, and it took off. It looked huge to me. It ran up behind the mainsail, as quick as that—" McCord snapped his fingers.

"Go on," I said. "What did you do then?"

"I followed the thing," he said. "I got up and went forward. I could see both sides of the deck. But when I got to the bow of the ship, all I found was—the cat.

"I'd had enough," he went on. "I aimed at the scar on her head and squeezed the trigger. It clicked on an empty shell. I was out of bullets.

"I headed for the cabin, and the cat followed me. Back in the cabin she went over to the water pan, but the pan was empty. And I had just put two quarts of water in it at sundown!"

He broke off again. "What's the use?" he said. "You didn't believe it when I said that someone—*something*—tried to lower the lifeboat. You think I'm drunk. But I tell you—"

He turned his head. Then he got up and moved toward the deck. He stood in the doorway, his head bent to the side. "Do you hear that?" he whispered.

"Hear what?" I said.

"Listen."

And then I heard it. It sounded like something had been lowered into the water with great care.

"You heard it?" McCord asked.

I went out on deck and looked over the side. "You see, there's nothing," I said. McCord was next to me, the lantern in his hand.

"Over there," he said, pointing toward the shore. "Something is swimming."

"It's probably just a breeze on the water," I said.

"Ridgeway! Look behind you!" I spun around quickly.

A yellow cat sat there on the deck.

We watched her for a moment. Then she turned and climbed the mast. She moved faster than any sailor could.

In an instant McCord was after her. I watched him climb the mast. Soon he was headed for the main topsail. A moment later he called down to me. "Heads up below!"

I ducked as something landed on the deck next to me. It was a straw slipper. Then another one landed next to it.

When McCord came down he was carrying two pistols, a Chinese kimono, and a cook's apron. "Well," he said, "I feel like a fool. I was starting to believe that stuff about the cat shifting souls!"

Back in the cabin McCord spoke first. "I'm glad the Chinaman got away. He's probably climbing up on shore, scared to death. I'd guess he's over near the oil tanks by now. Can you imagine how that poor man must feel, Ridgeway?"

"Yes," I said. "I think I can. He must have lost his nerve when he saw you heading for this ship. He hid in the topsails. And he took his cat with him."

"Yes," said McCord. "And he only came down because he needed water."

"Well, it looks like the mystery is solved," I announced.

McCord lifted his heavy eyelids. "The

mystery is that *I* didn't think of it. I've been at sea all my life. Yet I sailed around for three days with a man hiding in the topsail. And I didn't even realize—"

He shook his head. "When I think of him up there peeking down at me—" He rubbed at his eyes. "After all that, I could sure use some sleep."

"I should think so," I said, looking out toward the deck. McCord said nothing.

"By the way," I said, "I guess you were right about Bjornsen. He must have been starting to undo the topsail when the cat jumped out at him. Then he lost his balance and fell overboard. What do you think?"

Again McCord failed to answer. I turned to him. His head was hanging back over his chair and his mouth was opened wide. He was asleep.

Thinking About
the Stories

For They Know Not What They Do

1. What is the secret that Agnes Kain tries to keep from her son? Why is it important to her that he not learn the truth about his family? What *is* the truth about his heritage?

2. How long ago was this story written? Think about the readers of that time. How were their lives different from the lives of today's readers? Was their purpose for reading the same or different? Were their tastes in reading the same or different? In what ways?

3. Imagine that you have been asked to write a short review of this story. In one or two sentences, tell what the story is about and why someone would enjoy reading it.

Out of Exile

1. Who is narrating the story? Who are one or two of the minor characters? Describe each of these characters in one or two sentences.

2. Good writing always has an effect on the reader. How did you feel when you finished reading this story? Were you surprised, horrified, amused, sad, touched, or inspired? What elements in the story made you feel that way?

3. Suppose this story had a completely different outcome. Can you think of another effective ending for this story?

The Yellow Cat

1. Story ideas come from many sources. Do you think this story is drawn more from the author's imagination or from real-life experience? What clues in "About the Author" might support your opinion?

2. Look back at the illustration that introduces this story. What character or characters are pictured? What is happening in the scene? What clues does the picture give you about the time and place of the story?

3. Interesting story plots often have unexpected twists and turns. What surprises did you find in this story?